The
Secret
Kitten

Other titles by Holly Webb

The Snow Bear

The Reindeer Girl

The Winter Wolf

Animal Stories:

Lost in the Snow

Alfie all Alone

Lost in the Storm

Sam the Stolen Puppy

Max the Missing Puppy

Sky the Unwanted Kitten

Timmy in Trouble

Ginger the Stray Kitten

Harry the Homeless Puppy

Buttons the Runaway Puppy

Alone in the Night

Ellie the Homesick Puppy

Jess the Lonely Puppy

Misty the Abandoned Kitten

Oscar's Lonely Christmas

Lucy the Poorly Puppy

Smudge the Stolen Kitten

The Rescued Puppy

The Kitten Nobody Wanted

The Lost Puppy

The Frightened Kitten

The Secret Puppy

The Abandoned Puppy

The Missing Kitten

The Puppy who was Left Behind

The Kidnapped Kitten

The Scruffy Puppy

The Brave Kitten

The Forgotten Puppy

My Naughty Little Puppy:

A Home for Rascal

New Tricks for Rascal

Playtime for Rascal

Rascal's Sleepover Fun

Rascal's Seaside Adventure

Rascal's Festive Fun

Rascal the Star

Rascal and the Wedding

The Secret Kitten

Holly Webb
Illustrated by Sophy Williams

For Poppy and Star, my not-so-secret kittens...

www.hollywebbanimalstories.com

STRIPES PUBLISHING
An imprint of Little Tiger Press
1 The Coda Centre, 189 Munster Road,
London SW6 6AW

A paperback original
First published in Great Britain in 2015

Text copyright © Holly Webb, 2015
Illustrations copyright © Sophy Williams, 2015

ISBN: 978-1-84715-592-4

A CIP catalogue record for this book is available
from the British Library.

Printed and bound in the UK.

10 9 8 7 6 5 4 3 2 1

Chapter One

Lucy stood on tiptoe with her elbows balanced on the windowsill, leaning out to look down at the garden. She had never had a room like this before, right up at the very top of the house. She was so high up that the garden looked strange and far below, the trees short and stubby, even though she knew that they were tall.

Actually, she had never had a room of her own before. She had always shared with William, her little brother. But now they were living at Gran's house, there was space for each of them to have their own room. It was lovely and really odd, both at the same time.

Lucy had mixed feelings about everything at the moment. Gran's house was beautiful with a big garden, not like the tiny garden she'd had back home, but she couldn't stop thinking about the old house. They had been to Gran's loads of times, of course, but always as visitors. Living there was going to be strange and different. The house didn't feel like it was their home yet, even though Dad had explained that he'd bought half of it from Gran. They were all going to share. Gran would help look after Lucy and William, and Dad would sort out the wild, overgrown garden that had got too much for Gran recently, and they would all be company for each other.

It would be good for Dad, Lucy thought, resting her chin on her hands as she stared down at the trees. For the last five years, ever since their mum had died, he'd looked after her and William by himself. He'd had a little help from childminders, but mostly he had been in charge of everything. Now he would have Gran to help and maybe he wouldn't be so worried all the time. It was hard when he had to stay late at work and missed picking up Lucy and William from after-school clubs, or the childminder, or their friends' houses.

Lucy swallowed hard. They wouldn't be going back to their after-school clubs. They weren't even going back to their old school – Gran's house was too far away. On Monday, she and William would be starting all over again at a new school. Lucy wasn't looking forward to it.

"It'll be all right," Lucy whispered to herself. "It was nice when wc went to see it." The teacher had been friendly and smiley, William had loved the big climbing frame in the playground and it was only a five-minute walk from Gran's house. But it was new and different, and even though there would be a coat peg ready with her name on it and a drawer for her books in the classroom, Lucy knew she didn't really belong there, not yet.

Something stirred among the trees. Lucy squinted sideways, trying to work out what it was. A bird? Then she smiled. A large ginger cat was walking carefully along the fence, padding from paw to paw, slow and stately. He must belong next door, Lucy thought. Gran didn't have a cat. She didn't have any pets, even though this would be the perfect house for one with its lovely big garden. Lucy thought Gran's beautifully tidy living room would look a lot nicer with a cat draped along the back of the sofa, or curled up on the rug.

But Dad had told them that Gran didn't like pets. She thought they were too messy, and caused fuss and dirt and work. Lucy wished she could argue with Gran and say what about purring and how a cat could keep your feet warm on a cold night? But you couldn't start that sort of an argument with your gran – not her gran, anyway. She wasn't an arguing sort of person. Lucy loved her, but Gran was one of those people who knew she was always right. And she was the one who would be doing most of the tidying up, too!

"Lucy!"

It was William! Lucy spun round, hearing the wobbly tearful note in his voice. "What's the matter?" she asked worriedly.

"Gran shouted at me," William sniffed. He sat down on the floor, leaning against Lucy's bed. His face was muddy, except for two little trails where tears had run down.

"Why?" Lucy sat next to him and put her arm round his shoulders.

William snuggled into her. "I was playing football in the garden and then I brought the ball back in with me and I bounced it…"

"Oh, William! Where?" Lucy demanded and he edged away from her a little, hunching his shoulders up.

"In the living room."

"You didn't break anything, did you?" Lucy asked anxiously. Dad had made them promise to be careful, but William was only six and sometimes he just forgot things like that.

"No!" William protested indignantly. "But Gran was still really cross. She said I wasn't to kick balls around in the house, but I hadn't even kicked it! I was just bouncing it." He sighed and leaned back on her shoulder again, peering around Lucy's room at the cardboard boxes, already nearly all unpacked.

"Do you like having your own bedroom?" he whispered seriously.

Lucy nodded. "Yes... But last night I missed hearing you talking to your

Lego people," she added, to make him feel better.

"I do like my bedroom." William didn't sound so sure. "But do you think I could keep all my things in my room, then sleep up here with you? I could bring my sleeping bag."

"Maybe sometimes," Lucy said comfortingly. It had been strange going to bed last night without William snoring and snuffling on the other side of the room, but she was glad to have a place that was just her own.

All her own, except that it would be so nice to share it with a cat. Any cat, Lucy thought, wondering if the big ginger cat from next door ever came to visit.

Chapter Two

The black-and-white kitten peered around the pile of old boxes. Her ears were laid back flat and her tail was twitching. Out in the alleyway between the baker's shop and newsagent, she could see her brother and sister frisking about, chasing each other and wrestling. Her paws itched to join in. She stepped out a little further.

Then a car roared past on the
main road and she darted back into
her hiding place in the storage yard.
Seconds later, her tabby brother and
sister shot back in after her and they
all huddled together in the dark
little corner, hissing at the strange,
frightening noise. The two tabby
kittens wriggled and stamped their
paws inside a broken packing case,
making themselves comfy on the old
rags and torn-up papers, trying to find
the warmest, driest spot. The black-
and-white
kitten licked
them both
lovingly,
hoping that
they'd all curl

up together and snooze, as they waited
for their mother to come back from
her foraging. But the tabby kittens
didn't want to hide for long. A minute
or so later they were already nosing out
into the alleyway again.

Their little sister watched them
anxiously, wondering about that loud
noise and hoping that whatever it was
wouldn't come back. The alleyway was
so open – she liked places where she
could hide and still see everything. All
that space made her nervous.

"Oh, look! Kittens!"

A little boy came running into the
alleyway and the tabby kittens streaked
back towards the old boxes, knocking
their black-and-white sister sideways.
She huddled at the back of their little

den, her heart thumping, but the bravest of the tabbies was too curious to stay hidden, even with the boy blundering around, his feet stamping and thudding. She scrambled out past the broken board on to the top of the box and gazed at him.

"Mum, look…" the little boy whispered. "It really is a kitten! She's tiny!"

"Isn't she? She's gorgeous."

The black-and-white kitten squeaked worriedly. There was someone else out there, too. She wished her sister would come back, but now her brother was wriggling out to see what was going on.

"Oh, there's two! Look, Owen, the other one's come out to see you. I wonder who they belong to? I suppose they're strays, but they look very young. Their mother must be around somewhere."

The voices were soft and gentle, and the black-and-white kitten stretched her paws, shook her whiskers and began to creep towards the opening. Perhaps she would go and see what was happening.

But then the little boy shrieked with laughter, as kitten whiskers tickled his fingers. The kitten ran back and buried herself among the rags again. At last she heard their footsteps echoing back down the alleyway and she relaxed a bit. Then a tabby-striped face pushed in through the gap between the boxes and she darted forward to nuzzle happily at her mother. The thin tabby cat had been hiding out of the way until the little boy and his mum had gone. She had always been a stray and she wasn't very fond of people. People meant food, but sometimes they threw things and shouted at her for scrabbling around in bins. She avoided them as much as she could.

The tabby kittens piled in after her and tore at the ham sandwich she'd found for them, scrapping and hissing over the delicious pieces of ham. The kittens were eight weeks old and they were all still drinking her milk as well as eating food, but they were always hungry.

The black-and-white kitten finished her piece of sandwich and snuggled luxuriously up against her mother. She was warm and safe and full of food. Her brother and sister flopped down on top of her in a softly purring pile of fur and all four of them curled up to sleep.

"So, what was it like?" Gran asked, smiling at Lucy, as they walked home from school on Monday. She didn't need to ask how school had been for William. He was bouncing around the pavement in front of them with his new best friend, Harry, doing ninja kicks.

"It was all right," Lucy said, not very enthusiastically. It was true. No one had been mean and she'd understood the work they were doing. Emma, the girl who'd been told to look after her, had been nice and had made sure she knew where everything was.

But she'd stayed on the sidelines of all the games. And everyone knew secret jokes about the teachers that she didn't and there was no one who knew all the fun things about her, the things her friends back home knew. She was just a rather boring new girl.

Gran put an arm round her shoulders. "It'll get better, Lucy, I promise. In a month's time, it won't feel like a new school any more."

Lucy blinked. She hadn't expected Gran to notice that she wasn't really happy. "I suppose so," she murmured and smiled gratefully at Gran.

"Why don't we stop in at the baker's and get a treat? To celebrate school being just about all right?" Gran suggested.

William turned round mid-air and came racing back to them, saying goodbye to Harry. "Cakes? Can we?

Can I have a marshmallow ice cream?"

Gran made a face. "I suppose so.
I don't know how you can eat those
things, though."

"It's really easy," William told her
solemnly and Lucy giggled, feeling the
nervous lump inside her melt away for
the first time that day.

It was as they were coming out of the baker's shop, each clutching a rustling paper bag, that Lucy first saw the kittens. She wondered afterwards if they'd heard the bags crinkling, and were hoping that she and William might drop some food.

She'd seen a flash out of the corner of her eye, a darting movement in the alleyway. Lucy almost didn't stop to look at first – she'd thought that it was probably just pigeons, hopping about after crumbs – but then something had made her turn back and look properly.

The soft grey shadows peering out behind the bins had been cats!

No, kittens. Tiny kittens, two of them, their green eyes round and huge in little striped faces.

Lucy reached out her hand to grab at William, who was explaining very seriously to Gran that it was important to eat a marshmallow cone from the bottom up, as then you got to save the marshmallow for last.

"Ow! What?"

"Look…" Lucy whispered, pulling him closer so that he'd see. "But shh!"

"What am I looking at and you didn't have to grab me, Lucy, Dad says— Oh!"

Gran peered over their heads. "Please tell me that's not a rat."

"They're kittens, Gran. Can we go and take a closer look? Please?"

Gran looked at the shops on

either side of the alleyway. "Well, I shouldn't think they'll mind. Don't go into the yard, though, and don't touch them."

Lucy and William crept down the alley, holding hands. The little tabby kittens stared at them from behind the wheelie bins. They were crouched low to the ground, ready to spring away to safety, but they stayed still as the children came closer.

When they were almost at the bins, Lucy knelt down, gently pulling William with her.

"Can't we go closer?" he begged.

"Not yet," she whispered back. "When I went to Jessie's house, her cat was really shy and I had to sit like this for ages, but then he climbed into my lap and let me cuddle him. Jessie says he never does that." Suddenly, Lucy was blinking away tears, thinking of Jessie and all her friends back home.

"They're coming closer." William poked her arm impatiently. "Look!"

Lucy dragged her hand across her eyes. It was true – one of the kittens had padded all the way out now – he was almost close enough to sniff at William's outstretched fingers.

Then, all at once, he darted forward and dabbed his nose at William's hand.

William squeaked delightedly, "His nose is all cold and damp!"

The kitten disappeared back behind the bins in a blur.

"Sorry!" William whispered.

But it only took seconds for the kitten to be brave enough to peek out again, and this time the other tabby kitten followed him, sniffing curiously at Lucy's school shoes.

Very slowly, Lucy reached out and stroked the kitten's stripey head with the tips of her fingers – the fur was so soft, almost silky. And then the kitten purred, so loudly that Lucy couldn't help giggling. The noise seemed too big for such a tiny creature.

"I wonder where their mother is," Lucy murmured to William, looking down the alley to see if the mother cat was watching them playing with her babies.

"Are they lost?" William asked worriedly.

"No," Gran said quietly behind them. "I was just talking to Emma – the girl from the baker's. She said that they live in the yard – there's a pile of old boxes and things. She's been putting some food down for them."

"They live in a *box*?" Lucy said, thinking how cold it had been the night before.

Gran nodded. "Yes. But apparently a couple of her regular customers are thinking of trying to adopt these two, once they're big enough to leave their mother. That won't be long."

"Gran, there's another one!" Lucy gasped. "I was looking for their mum, but there's a kitten peeping out of that old box! A black-and-white one!"

"So there is!" Gran looked over to where Lucy was pointing. "That's odd, the lady in the shop only mentioned the two tabbies. Maybe that little one isn't as friendly as the others. I'm sorry, you two, we have to be off. I need to get dinner ready." She smiled down at Lucy's disappointed face. "I'm sure they'll still be here tomorrow…"

Chapter Three

They were late the next morning, because William had spilled half a bowl of cereal down his school uniform, so there was no time to stop and play with kittens. Lucy looked down the alleyway hopefully on their way to school, but she couldn't see even a whisker. She imagined all the kittens having a lie-in, curled up snugly in their old box.

When they stopped on the way home, Emma, the lady from the baker's, was there, putting some rubbish out in the bins. She smiled at Lucy and William and said, "Are you looking for those kittens? I'm really sorry, that lady I was telling your gran about came and took them home with her this morning."

"Oh…" Lucy swallowed. William's eyes had filled with tears and she felt like crying, too. She nudged her little brother. "That's good," she said firmly, trying to convince herself as well as William. "It's getting colder now it's autumn. Imagine sleeping outside in a box all winter."

Gran nodded. "It would be horrible. Damp and chilly. They're much better off with a nice home indoors."

"I know." William sniffed. "But I wanted to see them. We only got to see them once."

"I'll miss them," Emma said, as Lucy and William turned to go. "Cute little pair. Gorgeous stripes."

Lucy glanced back at her. "But – there was a black-and-white kitten, too. Did she take all three of them?"

Emma blinked. "Three? Really? I thought there were only two of them."

"No." Lucy shook her head. "Definitely three. We saw the black-and-white one yesterday."

"She's right," Gran put in. "I saw her, too. She reminded me of the cat I had when I was a little girl, called Catkin. This kitten had the same lovely white tip on her tail."

Lucy glanced at William in surprise. Gran had had a cat of her own? But she didn't like pets, Dad had said.

William wasn't really listening, though. "Gran, is the little kitten left all on her own now?"

"Her mum's still there," Emma pointed out.

"No other kittens to play with, though," Lucy said sadly.

William beamed at her. "Maybe she'll come and play with us instead, then, if she's lonely." He ran a few steps further down the alley and called, "Puss! Puss! Kitten!"

"She won't come out if you yell at her," Lucy said. "We've got to be gentle. Maybe tempt her out. Could we buy some cat treats, Gran?"

"I suppose so." Gran nodded. "Maybe if that kitten gets a bit more used to people, someone will take her home, too."

Lucy caught her breath. She almost asked Gran if they could be the ones to give the kitten a home. But then she remembered everything Dad had said about having to keep the house tidy and not damaging Gran's lovely things and how Gran hated mess. And then she thought about Jessie's mum rolling her eyes and sighing and saying, "Oh, not again!" when Jessie's cat Socks had knocked a vase of flowers off the kitchen table.

There was no way Gran would let them have a cat, even if the kitten did look like her old pet, Catkin.

Lucy frowned down at her magazine. It was her favourite one, a pet magazine that she got every week. She'd brought it into school to read at break time. Everyone was still being quite friendly, but she hated having to ask to join in the games. It was embarrassing. It was easier to sit on one of the benches and read.

This week's magazine had a big article on animal charities and an interview with the manager of a Cats Protection League shelter. She was talking about how important it was to find cats new homes quickly, as they didn't really like being kept all together. They wanted a place to call their own. Lucy sighed to herself as she thought of the black-and-white kitten.

But the really strange thing was that the Cats Protection League lady also said that black cats and black-and-white ones were much harder to find homes for than tabbies or gingers. Lucy just couldn't understand why. The article said that people thought black-and-white cats were a bit ordinary, not pretty like tabbies.

It made Lucy so cross that she almost tore the page, she was gripping it so tightly. How could people think that? All cats and kittens were different! Jessie's cat Socks was white, with a ginger tail and a funny ginger stripe down his nose. But that didn't mean he was a better pet than the little black-and-white kitten would be.

The article also said that some people didn't want cats that were black all over because they were worried that they might not be seen on the road, and could get run over. At least that made sense, Lucy thought. But they could always get their black cat a reflective collar, couldn't they?

"If I ever get a cat, I'm definitely

going to a shelter and choosing a black-and-white one," she murmured. "Or a lovely black cat. Like a witch's cat."

"Is it good?"

Lucy jumped so hard she nearly banged her head on the back of the bench and the girl leaning over to talk to her gasped.

"Sorry! I didn't mean to scare you. I get that magazine sometimes, too. I was just wondering if it was a good one this week."

"Oh!" Lucy nodded and smiled. "Yes. But sort of sad. There's a big bit about shelters. And it says not many people choose the black cats. I was just thinking I definitely would."

"Oh, me, too," the other girl agreed.

Lucy thought frantically, trying to

remember her name. There were loads of girls in her class, but she thought this one was called Sara. "Our cat's mostly black, but he's got a white front and white paws. My mum says he looks like he's wearing a penguin suit." She leaned over and looked at the article. "What's that about National Black Cat Day?"

Lucy looked at the bubble down near the bottom of the page. She hadn't got there yet. "The Cats Protection League invented it! To show everyone that black cats are special. It's in October – oh, the same day as Halloween. I suppose that makes sense. But black cats aren't all spooky."

Sara giggled. "They're good at appearing out of nowhere, though.

I'm always tripping over Harvey."

"Aw, that's such a cute name for a cat." Lucy smiled.

"He just looks like a Harvey," Sara explained. "Even when he was a kitten, there was something Harvey-ish about him. Have you got a cat?" she added, looking at Lucy sideways. There was something hopeful about the way she asked it, as though she wanted someone to share cat stories with. A friend who had a cat of her own – what could be better than that?

It was the first time someone had really seemed interested in her at school. If she said no, Sara would shrug and smile and walk away, Lucy was sure of it. And she was just as sure that she didn't want that to happen.

So she nodded, slowly, trying to think about what to say. "Yes. We've got a kitten." She slipped her hand under the magazine and crossed her fingers. She hated to lie, especially to someone as nice as Sara, but she had to. "We've only just got her." It was almost true, wasn't it? She wanted that little black-and-white kitten from the alleyway to be theirs, so much…

"Oh, you're so lucky! Is she gorgeous? What does she look like? How old is she?"

Lucy swallowed. "She's black and white, like Harvey. And she's very little, only just old enough to leave her mother. She was a stray."

"What's she called?" Sara demanded eagerly.

Lucy blinked. She couldn't think. Not a single name would come into her head. What was a good name for a kitten?

Then she smiled at Sara. She knew the perfect name, of course she did.

"She's called Catkin."

Chapter Four

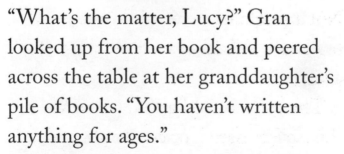

"What's the matter, Lucy?" Gran looked up from her book and peered across the table at her granddaughter's pile of books. "You haven't written anything for ages."

"It's a project." Lucy sighed. "It's difficult. It's about Egyptians and we can make the project about whatever we like – that's what's so hard about it.

I can't choose, even though I've got all these books out of the library."

And, of course, only half her mind was on her project. The rest of it was worrying about having lied to Sara two days ago. Especially as Sara was really, really excited. She kept asking about Catkin, and she obviously really wanted to come and see her. But she was too nice – or maybe too shy – to ask straight out if she could come round. Lucy had a feeling that she was working herself up to it, though.

The awful thing was, Lucy would have liked Sara to come round. She'd love to have a friend home for tea. Gran and Dad kept gently asking if there was anyone she really liked at school and if she wanted to invite somebody over. William had had Harry round and been back to his house, too. And he'd been invited to a birthday party already.

But if Sara came round, then she'd know that Lucy had been lying about Catkin and she'd hate her. She might even tell the entire class that Lucy was a liar.

"I went to Egypt, you know," Gran said thoughtfully, breaking into Lucy's thoughts. "It must have been, oh, goodness, eight, ten years ago? Yes, just before you were born, Lucy. We went to see the pyramids, me and one of my old schoolfriends. Auntie Barbara, you remember her?"

Lucy didn't, but she nodded as if she did. "You really went there? What was it like? Did you go and see the Great Pyramid?"

"We certainly did. We went inside it, as well. It was quite frightening," Gran added slowly. "Very shadowy and hard to breathe. I didn't like it much, Lucy, I have to admit, but I'm glad I saw it. And from the outside, they were incredible to look at. Wait a minute." She smiled and got up, walking through into the living room. Lucy could hear her opening drawers in the big display cabinet that had most of her precious, ever-so-breakable ornaments in it.

Gran came back in, carefully unrolling a piece of brownish paper. "Look, this is what I brought back as a souvenir of the holiday, Lucy.

It's a papyrus. Like paper, but made out of reeds." She held it out. "You can take it, have a look."

Lucy looked at her uncertainly. "Isn't it fragile?" she asked worriedly. She wanted to hold it – she could see that the painting on it was beautiful, a black cat wearing a jewelled necklace and even an earring, it looked like.

"I know you'll be careful." Gran smiled at her. "I ought to get it framed, really, it's such a lovely painting. The box at the side says my name in hieroglyphics. I watched the man doing it."

Lucy took the papyrus, feeling the roughness against her fingers. She could even see the lines of the reed stems in the weave. "The cat's so beautiful," she murmured. Then she grinned up at Gran. "I can't see many cats agreeing to wear all that jewellery, though. Most of them don't even like collars!"

Gran nodded. "But then she's a goddess, this one. Bast, she's called."

Lucy examined the picture again. "There was a cat goddess? Wow… Gran, I could make my project about her!" Very carefully, she laid the papyrus down on the table so she could fling her arms around her gran. "I could copy the painting, maybe. You're so clever!"

As she hugged Gran tightly, Lucy realized something else. Gran couldn't possibly dislike cats that much, could she? Not when she'd chosen a painting of a cat as a special souvenir.

The black-and-white kitten was enjoying a patch of sunlight in the yard. Her mother was off looking for food and the little kitten was stretched out, snoozing, with her nose on her paws.

Her ears fluttered a little as she caught a noise, coming from the back of one of the shops, and then her eyes snapped open. Someone was coming!

She darted back into the safety of the box den, her heart thudding fast against her ribs. The voices were loud, frightening even, and there were heavy feet clumping all around her.

She pressed herself back into the corner of the box, thinking that they would just dump their rubbish in the bins and go. But no one usually came close to the pile of old boxes like this. It wasn't a delivery – no van had driven down the alleyway. She was almost used to *that* noise, although she still didn't like it.

This was something different. And then suddenly the box, her safe, warm box, shifted and split and she let out a high-pitched squeak of fright. What was happening?

"There's something in there," a deep voice growled. "Ugh, not rats?"

"I don't think so – oh, there's a stray cat that hangs around the yard – perhaps it's her?"

Someone clapped their hands loudly, the sound sharp and echoing in the enclosed yard. "Go on, shoo! Off you go, cat!"

The kitten squeaked again and her box tipped sideways. She shot out, terrified, and streaked across the yard, away from the growling voices.

"There she goes – but that's just a kitten. Not much bigger than a rat, poor little thing!"

The kitten huddled in the corner, panicking. Someone was coming towards her, huge boots thumping. She had never tried to climb the fences before, but anything was better than staying here. She sank her claws in the wood and scrabbled frantically upwards, balancing for a moment on the very top of the fence. Then she jumped down the other side and set off through the bushes, who knew where.

Lucy was stretched out in the long grass, idly picking the blades. She'd done her homework and typed up loads of work for her project on the computer. She felt relaxed and happy in the autumn sun. Gran had given her a sandwich, to keep her going until Dad got home and they could all have dinner together, but Lucy hadn't finished it – she was feeling too lazy even to eat.

She could hear William right down the end of the garden, humming to himself as he investigated the greenhouse. Gran didn't use it very much these days and some of the glass panes were broken, but Dad had told them he'd plant seeds in the springtime. He'd already tidied up the bit of the garden nearest to the house, but Lucy and William loved this wild part, with the overgrown bushes. It was full of hidden nests and little dark caves. Lucy glanced sideways, checking that the big spotted garden spider hanging off the branch by her foot hadn't moved. She didn't mind him being there – he'd probably lived here longer than she had – but she didn't want him getting any closer.

He was still there. But underneath him, peering out at her from the shadows, was a tiny black-and-white face.

A kitten! The same kitten she had seen in the alleyway, Lucy was almost sure. She looked down the garden at the greenhouse and the fence. She hadn't realized before, but the shops were very close to the back of Gran's garden, even though to get to them by the street you had to go quite a way round.

"Did you climb over the fence?" Lucy whispered, very, very quietly.

The kitten stared back at her. She was very small and so thin, Lucy thought. She looked exhausted – as though she was frightened, but too worn out even to run.

Slowly, creeping her fingers across the grass, Lucy stretched out a hand to get her sandwich. It was chicken. Perfect for a kitten treat.

The kitten watched her, wide-eyed, shrinking back a little as Lucy's hand came close. But then she smelled the chicken – Lucy could see the exact moment. Her whiskers twitched and her ears flicked forward, then her eyes grew even rounder.

Lucy tore off a tiny piece of sandwich and gently laid it down, just where the tufts of long grass met the branches. Then she watched. The kitten didn't have to move far. If she wasn't brave enough, maybe Lucy could throw her a piece further in, but that might scare her away.

The kitten looked at the piece of sandwich and Lucy could see her sniffing. She looked between Lucy and the sandwich a few times, then she wriggled forwards on her stomach, inching slowly towards the food. As soon as she was close enough, she seized the chickeny mouthful and darted back into the safety of the bush.

Lucy wanted to laugh, but she folded her lips together firmly, in case the noise scared the kitten away. She watched the kitten wolf down the scrap and then she tore off a little more.

This time she left it a bit closer to her feet.

The kitten didn't take as long to decide she was going for the food the second time. She gave Lucy one slightly suspicious look and then raced to grab it.

After that, Lucy put the plate down, right next to her feet, to see what would happen. Surely the kitten wouldn't be able to drag away a whole sandwich, would she? She'd have to stop by the plate and eat it there. And then maybe Lucy would be able to stroke her…

The kitten stared at the sandwich. The two pieces she'd already eaten had been so delicious. But now the rest of the sandwich was closer to the girl and she wasn't sure that she was quite brave enough to go and take it.

But the smell… She could taste it in her mouth still and she was really hungry. She hadn't eaten for such a long time. After she had scrambled over the fence the afternoon before, she had run and climbed and run again, frightened and desperate to get away. Her cosy den in the box had suddenly been snatched from her and she didn't understand. She just knew that she wasn't safe there any more.

She had only stopped in the big garden because she was tired. Wriggling through the tiny gap under the back fence had worn her out. She had simply lain down in the dry, shadowy space under the bush and gone to sleep. When she'd woken, it had been dark and she had been so hungry. She'd finally understood that everything was different now. Her mother wasn't there to bring her food and there was no one there to curl up and sleep with. She was lost and all alone.

She had been on her own before, of course she had. But she had always known that her mother would come back. The kitten would purr throatily, and her mother would wash her, licking her fur lovingly all over.

Now her fur was dusty and matted with dirt, and a clump of it had torn out when she had squeezed under the fence. She had sat there below the bush and tried to wash herself, but it wasn't the same and it only made her feel more lonely.

The night sounds seemed louder than they'd ever been before. Cars roared past and made her shudder with fright, and people laughed and shouted. Another cat had stalked through the garden, late at night, but it hadn't been her mother. She had jumped up eagerly, ready to run and nuzzle it, but all it had done was stare at her and she'd seen it thicken out its tail. Then it had paced on, away down the side of the house and the kitten had ducked back under the bush, knowing that she was more lost than ever.

As Lucy pursed her lips and tried to make kitten-encouraging noises that sounded something like *prrrrrp*, the kitten stared back at her and wondered what to do. The girl seemed quiet and gentle, not like those stomping men that had chased her away from her home. And she had food. Just now, food seemed the most important thing of all.

Slowly, paw by paw, the kitten came out of her hiding place and crept towards Lucy.

Chapter Five

"Lucy…"

"*Shh!*"

"Lucy, is that a kitten? Is that the kitten from by the baker's shop?"

"Yes, but *shh!* Please don't make her run away. She's really shy, William. Look, come and sit down here."

William sat down, as slowly and quietly as he could, and stared at the kitten. She stared back for a moment, but she was so busy devouring the rest of the chicken sandwich that she didn't really have time to worry about him.

"How did she get here?"

"I don't know." Lucy reached out one hand and held it by the plate, close enough for the kitten to sniff. The kitten glared at her and then butted gently at Lucy's hand.

William giggled. "She's telling you to get off her sandwich."

"Maybe. Or she might be putting her scent on me," said Lucy. "That's what a cat's doing when it rubs its face against you. They've got scent glands there. They're saying we belong to them." *I want to belong to you*, she added silently. *Please stay. Please, please, please.*

"Lucy," William whispered. "Do you think – do you think she could be our cat? Can we keep her?" He looked around the garden. "We could make her a nest in the greenhouse. Wow, she's actually finished all of that sandwich. Do you think she wants another one? Gran asked if I wanted a sandwich but I said no. I could go and say that I've changed my mind…"

Lucy looked worried. "I don't like

telling Gran lies – but we can't tell her the truth, can we? Dad said she wouldn't want a pet in the house. And this kitten really needs food. She's so skinny."

"The greenhouse isn't the same as being in the house," William pointed out. "I bet she wouldn't mind. So it doesn't matter if we don't tell her."

Lucy couldn't help thinking that it *did* matter, and that they were just twisting things around to be the way they wanted – but she wouldn't be able to bear it if Gran made them take the kitten back to the alleyway. The greenhouse would be like a palace to a kitten who was used to living in a box. And Gran didn't usually go down to the end of the garden. It would be all right.

And if she really had a kitten, she wouldn't be lying to Sara any more.

"Yes." She nodded. "Go and ask Gran if you can have a sandwich. With lots of chicken."

"Oh dear, what's the matter with that poor little girl?" Gran speeded up as they made their way home from school. She hurried down the pavement towards a toddler, standing outside the baker's shop next to a little scooter and howling. "I hope she's not lost."

"She isn't, Gran, look, I can see her mum coming." Lucy pointed to a lady running towards the little girl.

"Good." Gran bent over the little

girl. "What happened, sweetheart? Did you fall off your scooter?"

The little girl stared back at her and shook her head. She stopped crying.

Gran smiled at the little girl's mother, who had reached them at last and was now crouched next to her daughter, hugging her and all out of breath. "I'm sorry, we didn't see what happened, but she says she didn't fall."

"Mummy! The cat!" And the little girl began to howl again.

"Oh, Macey! Did you try and stroke a cat? Did he scratch you?"

The little girl nodded and wailed louder, holding up her arm towards her mum.

Lucy sucked in her breath through her teeth – Macey had a long scratch down the inside of her arm. It wasn't bleeding very much, but it obviously hurt.

"Some cats are just grumpy, Macey. You know I said not to chase after them." Her mum sighed. "Don't worry, baby. We'll go home and put one of your teddy-bear plasters on it."

Lucy bit her lip. It probably wasn't the right time to say that the cat must have been scared if the little girl had tried to grab it.

"It was probably that stray tabby that lives down the end of the alleyway," Gran said. "Stray cats can be very wild and fierce."

Lucy and William exchanged glances, thinking of the little black-and-white kitten, curled up in the greenhouse back at home. They'd made her a cosy nest out of one of the cardboard boxes they'd had for packing up their things, tipped on its side and lined with an old sweatshirt of Lucy's. Then they'd laid the kitten a trail of chicken sandwich pieces to show her where the greenhouse was.

Lucy and William had done their best to make it into the nicest den a kitten could have. They'd even made her a litter tray, out of an old seed tray they'd found on one of the greenhouse shelves – it had been full of dusty earth. Lucy had a feeling the kitten might not know what it was for, as she was a stray and used to weeing anywhere, but if she was going to be an indoor cat one day, it was important to try. William had brought her a plant saucer full of water from the outside tap, as well.

That morning, before they went to school, Lucy had nipped out with some Weetabix and milk. It wasn't the best thing for a kitten, she knew, but they didn't have any proper cat food. Anyway, the kitten hadn't seemed to mind. She had buried her face in it eagerly and when Lucy finally had to go, the kitten had been blissfully licking milky gunge off her whiskers.

She hadn't looked very wild and fierce at all. She was still shy, of course. But when Lucy had arrived with the bowl, she hadn't run away, or hidden herself behind the wobbly towers of flowerpots. Instead, she'd just pricked her ears, wary, but hopeful.

Lucy and William lagged behind Gran for the rest of the way home. "Did you hear what Gran said about stray cats being fierce?" William asked anxiously.

Lucy nodded. "I know. I was really wishing we could tell her about Catkin."

"Catkin?" William blinked in surprise. "You named her?" He frowned a little. Lucy could tell he was hurt that she'd given the kitten a name without talking to him.

"Gran used to have a black-and-white cat called Catkin," Lucy explained. "She was telling me about her. It's a really sweet name and I thought that maybe if we called the kitten Catkin, too, it would remind her of it. But now Gran's thinking about nasty fierce cats instead. It's the worst timing ever."

"Ohhh." William nodded. "I see. But our Catkin's sweet, Lucy. She's not fierce at all. Gran will see that, won't she?"

"Mmmm. But let's not tell her just yet that we've got Catkin in the greenhouse. She'll have to go on being our secret kitten. And don't tell Dad, either!"

"Come on, you two!" Gran called back. "It's starting to rain."

Lucy and William sped up, the first fat drops splashing on to the pavement as they dashed after Gran.

"What if she gets wet?" William hissed. "The greenhouse has got all those big holes in the roof! She'll get wet!"

"You're right," Lucy muttered back. She smiled at William. "You know that big old wardrobe in my bedroom… Perhaps we could hide her in there?"

"Why not my bedroom?" William said.

"Because you haven't got a wardrobe, just drawers. And because your bedroom's next to Dad's! Mine's up those creaky stairs and I can always hear people coming. So I've got time to hide a kitten in my wardrobe before they get to the top, you see?"

"I suppose so." William sighed heavily.

Lucy smiled to herself, imagining falling asleep tonight with the faint sound of purring echoing out from her wardrobe. Or maybe even a small furry ball of kitten on the end of her bed. "I hope she understands we're trying to help," Lucy said suddenly. "She might not want to come inside.

She's probably never been in a house before." Lucy had thought they'd be able to tempt Catkin inside gradually. She'd never thought of doing it so soon.

William grinned at her. "I think if you gave her a chicken sandwich she'd probably go anywhere!"

Chapter Six

"Distract Gran! Show her your cut knee," Lucy muttered, thinking of Macey and her scratch. She had the wet kitten and her old sweatshirt bundled up in her arms and there was a lot of squeaking and wriggling going on. She'd taken the cold sausages from her lunch box (she'd saved them on purpose) and they'd nipped outside while Gran was taking off her coat and changing into her slippers. Catkin had been so excited about the sausages, she'd hardly minded when Lucy had picked her up. But now Lucy needed a clear run upstairs. "Go in the utility room… Pretend you're looking for the first-aid box. Quick!" The armful of sweatshirt was wriggling like mad. "It's all right, Catkin. Just a tiny bit longer."

William nipped in through the back door and then into the utility room. If he could get Gran to follow him in there, she wouldn't see Lucy dash past.

"Gran! My knee's bleeding! Can you get me a plaster? I fell over at school."

Lucy could hear Gran bustling through the kitchen and then the squeak of the utility-room door. It was on Dad's DIY list to oil that door, so she was glad he hadn't done it yet. Huddling Catkin close, she darted through the kitchen, into the hallway and up the stairs.

Up in her room, she kicked the door gently shut and put her bundle down on the floor. Catkin shook her way out of the sweatshirt looking indignant and hissed faintly at Lucy.

"Sorry," Lucy whispered back.
"I couldn't let Gran see you. And it's
really pouring with rain out there now.
I bet your box is soggy already. I'll
make you a new bed, look."

She grabbed another cardboard box
off the teetering pile in the corner of
her room and put it sideways in the
bottom of her wardrobe, shoving all
her shoes to one side. Catkin was still
standing on the sweatshirt, so Lucy
made a nest shape out of her woolly
winter scarf and put that in the box
instead. Then she put the last half of
sausage down in front of the box, too.
It was still sitting in one of Gran's

neat little plastic lunch pots, which made a perfect cat-food bowl.

"I'll get you some water in a minute," Lucy promised. "And the litter tray. Your things are just outside the back door. William brought them in from the greenhouse."

She looked at her kitten home thoughtfully and then at Catkin, who had slunk under her bed. The kitten looked worried.

"I know it's strange," Lucy told her quietly. "But we're nice. Really. And there's more sausage, look." She tapped her fingernails against the wardrobe door to make Catkin look and then tipped up the lunch pot to show her. "Did you want another chicken sandwich instead? Are they your favourite? They're my favourite, too."

Catkin edged out from under the bed, sniffing. She was confused. But she had never had so much food before – her brother and sister had always fought for more of their mother's milk and the same with the scraps. It wasn't just the sandwiches and the cereal or the sausages, either – the two children had been so gentle. Lucy and William had whispered to her and tried to purr at her and that morning Lucy had run one finger softly all down her back, which had made her quiver. It had been strange and different, but she had liked it. And now there was another soft box bed and more food. She liked being inside, all warm and dry. So she padded cautiously across the room and stopped to sniff at Lucy's fingers. Then she butted her head up against Lucy's hand and went to nibble daintily at the sausage in the pot.

Lucy sat watching her, smiling to herself. Her own kitten. In her own bedroom. Almost, anyway.

Then she froze. The steps up to her room were creaking. She was just sitting forward, ready to scoop Catkin further into the wardrobe and close the door, when she heard William hissing, "It's only me! I've got the tray!"

Lucy wriggled back slowly and went to open the door. "You star! How did you do that?"

"Gran's on the phone to Auntie Susie. She'll be ages. Angel Katie got a distinction in her ballet exam." Angel Katie was what they called their perfect little cousin. "Gran was in the living room and she didn't see me at all. I've got the water, too."

"That's brilliant. Look, if I move my shoes and put them under my desk instead, we can put the litter tray in the corner of the wardrobe. And this newspaper I used to wrap my photo frames can go underneath, just in case. Don't worry, Catkin. We're just making it nice for you."

"I hope she understands what to do," William said doubtfully. "What if she wees in the wrong place? Like, I don't know, in your slippers?"

Lucy grinned at him. "Yuck. But actually, I don't think I'd mind. She's only little. I remember when you were a baby and you weed in Dad's face when he was changing your nappy."

William went scarlet. "You don't! You can't remember that, you were only little yourself."

"Well, I remember Dad telling me about it once, anyway. I bet Catkin won't make as much mess as a baby."

Catkin finished the sausage and sniffed thoughtfully at the litter tray. Then she snuggled up on Lucy's scarf and pulled the sweater over herself, almost like a blanket. She tucked her nose comfortably under her tail and, as the two children watched, she fell fast asleep.

"I hope Gran didn't go into your room for anything today," William whispered to Lucy, as they hurried across the playground the next afternoon. It was Friday and everyone was running and swinging their bags, eager to get home and start the weekend.

"Me, too. But I don't think she would have done. I took all of my washing downstairs and put it in the machine for her. And Dad vacuumed my room a couple of days ago. Catkin was really good last night. She didn't mew or anything, and she even used the litter tray. This morning she was sitting on my windowsill when I woke up, just looking out of the window."

Lucy crossed her fingers. "Look, there's Gran by the gate. She doesn't look cross, does she? Not like someone who's found a kitten in a wardrobe." They waved to Gran and she waved back, smiling.

Just then someone called out her name, "Lucy!" It was Sara.

Lucy swung round and beamed at her friend. "Hello!"

"Lucy, can I ask you a big favour?" Sara said pleadingly, as they walked towards the gate. "I live quite close to you, you know. Just a couple of streets further on. Do you think I could pop into your house for five minutes on the way home? Just to see your gorgeous kitten? Pleeease? My mum said it was fine if you said I could."

Lucy stopped walking and swallowed hard. She so wanted to say yes. Perhaps she could even tell Sara the secret. But there wasn't time. Gran would hear them, she was really close. In fact, she was coming towards them, smiling. She was probably about to invite Sara to come for tea.

"I-I can't today…" Lucy whispered, her eyes darting sideways at Gran. "I've got – dancing." Gran had been talking about signing her up for dance classes – there were some at the church hall, not far away. It was the first thing that came into her head.

It was just a pity that William blurted out, "I've got to go to football!" at the same time.

"We've got both," Lucy said hurriedly.

"It's just not a good day, Friday."

Gran was standing beside them now, looking curious, and Lucy could see Sara's mum coming over, too.

"If you don't want me to come—" Sara started to say, sounding a bit hurt.

"It isn't that! I do want you to, I really do!"

"You just had to say no – I thought we were friends!"

"We are!" Lucy said anxiously. "It's just – not today. Another day!"

Sara nodded, but she still looked really disappointed. She grabbed her mum's hand and pulled her away down the street, leaving Lucy and William and Gran staring at each other in confusion.

"Lucy, whatever's the matter? Wasn't that Sara, that nice girl who lives on Foxglove Way? Have you fallen out with her?"

"Yes." Lucy sniffed. "She wanted to come to our house."

"Well, why didn't you let her? She could have had dinner with us."

"It wasn't that. I can't explain. Please can we go home?" Lucy reached out and took Gran's hand. "Please."

"All right." But Gran still sounded worried and she kept hold of Lucy's hand as they walked on. Lucy could tell she hadn't finished asking about what had happened. "Lucy, was Sara asking about a kitten?" she said at last, as they walked past the alleyway. "I thought I heard her say something about visiting a kitten…"

Lucy swallowed. "But we haven't got a kitten," she pointed out, trying to sound cheerful.

"Lucy…" Gran pulled her hand gently to make her stop. "Just go on ahead for a minute, William. Look, you can take my keys. Go and open the front door. We'll follow you." She watched as William walked on ahead and then she followed, walking along slowly with Lucy's hand held tight in hers. "Lucy, did you tell Sara you had a kitten?"

Lucy didn't say anything. How could she explain?

Gran went on thoughtfully. "Sometimes it's hard, when you really want to make friends – you make up stories. Little stories to make yourself sound more interesting. Everyone does it sometimes, Lucy, it's all right."

Lucy gaped up at her. "How did you know?"

"Like I said, everyone does it. But almost everyone gets found out, too, Lucy love. You're going to have to explain to Sara and say you're sorry, you know."

Lucy kicked at the pavement with her foot. "I know," she muttered. But inside she was saying, *I didn't make it up. It wasn't a lie. Well, it was when I first said it. But now I'm lying to you instead… I wish we'd told you about Catkin in the first place. What am I going to do?*

"Are you that desperate for a kitten?" Gran asked suddenly.

Lucy blinked, shocked out of her worries. "Um. I would love one. But Dad said you didn't like pets. Because they were dirty."

Gran sniffed. "Well, I do like everything to be clean," she agreed. "But a little cat… Maybe we could think about it."

Lucy swallowed hard and tried to smile. Somehow she had to explain to Gran that they had a little cat already…

When they got back to the house, Gran made hot chocolate and she even put marshmallows on the top, as a treat. She let Lucy and William take it upstairs, though she did say they had to be careful not to spill any.

"Dinner will be in about an hour," she reminded them. "Your dad's working late tonight, so we're not waiting for him today."

Lucy and William carried the hot chocolate upstairs to Lucy's room, with the sandwiches they'd both saved from lunch. At the top of the steps, outside the door, they stopped and looked at each other worriedly. Somehow Lucy felt convinced that the kitten wouldn't be there. Perhaps they had imagined it all. She reached out and turned the handle, peering cautiously around the door.

Over in the wardrobe, the kitten lifted her head and yawned. Then she looked up at them and nosed at the empty plastic pot, clearly hoping for some tea.

"Hello," Lucy whispered, starting to shred up her sandwich. "Did you miss us?"

Catkin yawned again and, very faintly, Lucy heard her purr.

"You're pleased to see us! You're actually purring. Oh, Catkin. If only we could show you to Gran right now, I'm sure she'd want to keep you." She patted Catkin's head, loving the feeling of the silky fur under her fingers. "This weekend, somehow, we'll find a way to tell her. We have to."

Chapter Seven

When Lucy and William's dad got home late that night, he sat across the kitchen table from their gran, eating his dinner.

"What's the matter?" he asked, as he wiped a bit of bread round his plate to mop up the gravy. "You've hardly said anything since I got home, Mum."

Gran sighed and put down her mug

of tea. "I'm just a bit worried about Lucy. I'm not sure she's settling all that well with the other girls at school. She had a bit of an argument with one of them this afternoon, just as I was picking her up. She didn't want to talk about it very much, but it seems as though she'd told this girl – Sara, her name is – that we had a kitten."

Dad stared at her. "But why on earth would she say that?"

Gran shrugged. "To fit in? To make herself a bit more exciting? We're asking a lot of them, you know, starting at a new school."

Dad's shoulders slumped. "I suppose so. But I thought it was the best thing to do…"

"I still think it is." Gran reached over and patted his hand. "But I'm wondering if a pet would help Lucy settle."

"You don't like pets!"

"Whatever gave you that idea? I wouldn't want a dog, I couldn't manage the walking, but I love cats!" Gran smiled at him, a little sadly. "Actually, I suppose we didn't have any pets when you were younger, did we? I haven't had a cat of my own for a long time.

Not since Catkin died. He was twenty, you know, and I'd had him since I was a little girl. I didn't want another cat for a while after that and somehow then it just never seemed to be the right time. But I wouldn't mind a cat now. Especially with Lucy and Wiliam to help look after it."

"Well, it would be wonderful for Lucy," Dad agreed. "I always said no before, because we were out of the house all the time." He got up and took his plate over to the dishwasher. "I'll go and check on her. I know she'll probably be asleep, but I just want to see that she's all right…"

Catkin woke up as the morning light shone into Lucy's room. She didn't have any blinds yet and the morning was bright and sunny. The kitten stretched blissfully, padding her paws into a patch of sun just outside the wardrobe. Then she hunched up the other way, arching her back like a spitting witch's cat and stepped delicately out into Lucy's bedroom.

Lucy was still fast asleep, huddled up under her duvet, so Catkin jumped up on to the bed to sniff at her. She smelled interesting, like breakfast and warm sunshine. But she didn't wake up when Catkin dabbed a chilly nose against her ear – only muttered and turned over, which made the duvet shift alarmingly. Catkin sprang down before she slid off and sat on the rug.

When she'd washed her ears
thoroughly, both sides, she stalked
off across the room. Something
was different and she hadn't quite
worked out what it was. There was
something in the air, something fresh
and new.

The door was open!

Lucy had shut it carefully, of course,

when she came upstairs to bed. But then her dad had come up to check on her. Catkin and Lucy had both been fast asleep and neither of them had seen that he had left the door ajar. Just wide enough for a small, determined paw to hook it open.

Catkin nosed her way out and started to hop carefully – front feet, then back feet – down the stairs. It felt unfamiliar. Then she trotted along the landing, sniffing curiously at the different doors. She padded into William's room, but a wobbly pile of books slid over when she nudged it, so she darted out again and set off down the next flight of stairs to the bottom. She sniffed her way carefully down the hallway and into the kitchen.

Most of the food was shut away in cupboards, but Dad had left a loaf of bread out on the counter and Catkin could smell it. She sat on the floor, staring up and thinking…

Lucy woke up when the sunny patch from the window moved round on to her bed. She blinked sleepily, wondering why it was that she felt so happy and scared all at the same time. Then she sat up straight, remembering.

Catkin!

Today they *had* to find a way to tell Gran and Dad what had happened, and make them see that Catkin needed to stay with them.

The kitten wasn't sitting on the windowsill the way she had been the day before, so Lucy kneeled up in bed and leaned over to peer into the wardrobe. "Catkin," she called. "Puss, puss, puss…"

But no little kitten face appeared and Lucy's heart began to beat faster. "Where did you go?" she murmured. She hopped out of bed and crouched down to check underneath, but there was nothing there except dust. No Catkin hiding in the cardboard boxes, or behind the little bookshelf by the door.

The open door.

Lucy gasped. "I shut it!" she whispered to herself. "I know I did. Oh no." She hurried down the stairs,

going as fast as she could on tiptoe,
so as not to wake Dad or Gran. She
dashed into William's room.

"Wake up! William, wake up! Have
you seen Catkin? I don't know where
she is."

William stared at her sleepily,
blinking like an owl, and then he
squeaked and jumped out of bed.

"Where would she go?"

"Shh! I don't know, maybe the kitchen?"

William nodded. "Definitely the kitchen."

They hurried down the stairs, freezing to a stop every time one of them creaked. The house was old and they hadn't had time to learn which stairs to step over.

"Dad'll hear us," Lucy whispered miserably. "Hurry up, we have to find her and get her back into my room." She kneeled down on the kitchen floor, looking around. She hadn't noticed how many tiny, kitten-sized hiding places there were in here before. On the chairs, under the table. Down the side of the oven. "Oh! What if she's climbed into the washing machine?" Lucy gasped. "I read about a cat who did that once."

But the washing machine was empty and so were all the other spots they could think of. Lucy sat down on the floor, looking helpless. "I can't think of anywhere else," she murmured. "All the windows are closed, aren't they?"

William nodded. "It was cold last night. Unless – Gran always sleeps with her bedroom window open."

A large tear spilled down the side of Lucy's nose. "Maybe she went out that way, then. She didn't want to stay. Catkin's gone!"

Chapter Eight

"Whatever's the matter with you two? Why are you up at seven o'clock on a Saturday morning?" Gran demanded. She was standing in the kitchen doorway, wrapped in her dressing gown. "Lucy, you're crying! What's wrong?" She put her arms around Lucy, pulling her up from the floor.

"We've lost her!" Lucy sobbed into

Gran's shoulder. She didn't care about keeping Catkin a secret any more. It was too late now.

"Lost who?" Gran stared at Lucy in puzzlement and so did Dad, who'd come in behind her, looking sleepy.

"Catkin," William explained, coming to lean against Dad's dressing gown. "Our kitten. Lucy found her in the garden. She was in Lucy's wardrobe, but when we woke up she'd gone."

"You had a kitten shut in your wardrobe?" Dad said slowly.

"Not shut in," Lucy shook her head, gulping back tears. "Just her bed was in there and her litter tray. She could go anywhere in my room. We couldn't leave her in the greenhouse – the glass is full of holes and it was pouring with rain on Thursday night."

Dad and Gran looked shocked. "But what were you feeding her?" Gran asked, frowning.

"Sandwiches, mostly. She loves chicken." Lucy sniffed. "Just like me. We saved bits of our lunches for her and she was getting tame. We thought she was going to stay with us, but now she's run away. She must have gone through your window, Gran. It's the only one that was open." Lucy slumped down on one of the kitchen chairs.

Gran moved slowly over to the counter to put the kettle on, tidying away the breadcrumbs and pushing shut a half-open drawer on the way. "I need a cup of tea," she murmured. "A kitten in your wardrobe…"

"Where did she come from in the first place? That's what I want to know," Dad said, sitting down opposite Lucy with William on his knee.

"The alley down by the baker's," Lucy explained tiredly. "There were three of them – the two tabbies got adopted, but nobody cared about the little black-and-white kitten. And then she just turned up in our garden."

"And you named her Catkin? Like my Catkin?" Gran asked, getting mugs out of the cupboard.

"You said your kitten was black and white, too," Lucy explained. "And it's a sweet name. It was just right."

"Oh dear," Gran sighed. "Perhaps she was just too wild to be a pet, Lucy. If she's never really known people…"

"But she wasn't wild," Lucy tried to explain. She could feel herself starting to cry again. "She was shy, but she purred at us. And she loved our food, even if she didn't really love us yet."

"Well, perhaps we could go back to the alley by the shops and look for her," Gran said thoughtfully, leaning over to get a clean tea towel out of the drawer.

"You mean – if we found her we could bring her back home again?" Lucy gasped. "We can keep her?" She jumped up. "Can we go round there now?"

William wriggled off Dad's knee. "Right now?"

But Gran was standing staring into the tea-towel drawer. "I don't think we need to… Look."

Lucy leaned over and clapped her hand across her mouth. Curled up in among Gran's neatly ironed tea towels was a black-and-white kitten, half-asleep and blinking up at them in confusion.

"I shut the drawer…" Gran murmured.

"When I went to make the tea. It was open, just a little. You know how that drawer sticks sometimes…"

"Just enough for a skinny kitten to climb in, but not enough for us to see her!" Lucy said, her eyes wide.

Sleepily, Catkin stared up at Lucy and Gran and let out a little purr. Perhaps there was going to be food. The bread seemed a long while ago and it had been a lot of effort to get up on to the counter and steal a slice. She was hungry again.

"What a sweetheart," Gran said, laughing as Catkin stepped carefully out of her nest in the drawer. She rubbed her furry face against Gran's hand and purred even louder. "Just like my Catkin," Gran said, petting her ears. "You're staying now, are you?"

Catkin jumped down to the floor and wove her way round Gran's ankles and then Lucy's, still purring.

"That means yes," Lucy whispered. "I know it does."

"You actually had her hidden in your wardrobe?" Sara asked Lucy again, as they followed Gran home from school on Monday afternoon. "You had a secret kitten?"

"Yes. And I really wanted you to see her, but I couldn't let Gran find out. Or I thought I couldn't. It turns out we probably should have just told her to start with."

"That wouldn't have been as exciting," Sara said, shaking her head.

"No." Lucy smiled at her. "It *was* lovely, Catkin being our secret. But now we can play with her without worrying about Dad and Gran. And she still likes my bedroom best in all of the house."

"Shall we pop in and buy a cake for after tea, girls?" Gran suggested, stopping as they reached the baker's. "Oh, William, come back!"

Lucy and Sara giggled as William raced ahead, flinging open the door of the baker's. When they caught up with him, he was already telling Emma behind the counter that he wanted a marshmallow ice cream.

"You know the black-and-white

kitten, the one that was living in your yard?" Lucy said shyly to Emma, after they'd chosen their cakes. "She came into our garden and we're going to keep her!"

Emma smiled delightedly. "Oh, that's such good news! I looked for her, after you two told me she was there, but I never saw her. I did wonder if you'd imagined her."

"No, she's just a bit shy." Lucy smiled to herself, remembering Catkin chasing madly round the kitchen after a ping-pong ball that morning and then collapsing in her lap, exhausted, with her paws in the air. She wasn't shy with them, not any more.

"I've got news for you, too," Emma went on, as she put their chocolate doughnuts into a bag. "I called the cat shelter about the kittens' mum, to ask them what the best thing was to do. They're going to catch her and spay her so she doesn't have more kittens. They said she probably won't ever be tame enough to be a house cat, but if she's not trying to feed kittens all the time she'll be a lot less thin and worried, poor thing. So they'll bring her back and she can live in the yard. We'll put scraps out for her."

"Thank you!" Lucy forgot to be shy and gave Emma a hug. "You're amazing. I never even thought of doing that!"

"Maybe Catkin can come back and visit her," William suggested, reaching into his bag and picking the hundreds and thousands off his marshmallow ice cream.

"Maybe." Lucy smiled, imagining the two cats nose to nose, sniffing hello. All of a sudden she couldn't wait to get home and see Catkin and show her off to Sara, too.

Her own kitten, not-so-secret any more…